UNDERSTANDING APOSTOLIC MISSIONS

Or The Call into Missions

ABOUT THE BOOK

This book is written to inspire, instruct, teach, educate and encourage everyone who desires to serve God at one capacity or the other, especially as a missionary. It contains examples, true life stories, pictures and testimonies. I am positive that an encounter with this book would equip you adequately, leave you inspired, enlightened and fired up to expand the frontiers of God's kingdom God bless you as you read.

So, Who is a Missionary?

Let's be quick to note that missionary work is generic and not the same everywhere. This clarification becomes imperative because the work of a missionary has been stereotyped and interpreted to be same and one thing especially because the early missionaries did it in a certain way, does not mean it has to remain the same everywhere and forever.

From the word missionary, a missionary is someone or a set of people on a specific mission from one place sent to another region to fulfill a specific mission, in the light of the gospel. A missionary goes out to spread and advance the kingdom of God in a virgin land (a place where the gospel is not known or have not been preached or where people have not properly received Jesus as Lord. A missionary is someone who is sent on an assignment (mission) by God, especially, to do religious or charitable work in a different territory.

Stories have been told and read about how early foreign missionaries to Africa and Asia risked their lives based on limited health knowledge and technology which could have prevented certain sicknesses and diseases. Unfortunately, the diseases ravaged and killed a lot of the

Missionaries sent to Nigeria and many died of malaria fever because of exposure to mosquito bites. Many also suffered from lack of adequate funding while others suffered from hostile cultures and traditions. However, apart from Africa, missionaries were sent to continents and countries like Asia, India, Pakistan, Malaysia etc.

The book of Act 13:4 reveals one of the missionary journeys of Paul:

Paul's First Missionary Journey

4 So Barnabas and Saul were sent out by the Holy Spirit. They went down to the seaport of Seleucia and then sailed for the island of Cyprus. 5 There, in the town of Salamis, they went to the Jewish synagogues and preached the word of God. John Mark went with them as their assistant.6 Afterward they traveled from town to town across the entire island until finally they reached Paphos, where they met a Jewish sorcerer, a false prophet named Bar-

Jesus. 7 He had attached himself to the governor, Sergius Paulus, who was an intelligent man. The governor invited Barnabas and Saul to visit him, for he wanted to hear the word of God. 8 But Elymas, the sorcerer (as his name means in Greek), interfered and urged the governor to pay no attention to what Barnabas and Saul said. He was trying to keep the governor from believing.

Table Of Contents

A MISSION ASSIGNMENT

Usually, a mission assignment is a situation where a missionary or a group of missionaries travel to a foreign land and stay there for a couple of years or for the rest of their lives. As much as this is a great cause, it should not be copied without first confirming from the Lord, to be sure if that is the nature of the mission one is sent to do because there are diversities in missions. Scriptures make it clear that there was a mission that Apostle was involved in and he had to stay in the place for two full years.

ACT 28:30-31

30 Paul stayed there two full years in his own rented house, welcoming all who came to visit him. 31Boldly and freely he proclaimed the kingdom of God and taught about the Lord Jesus Christ....

HOW LONG DOES A MISSION REQUIRE?

Here is one of the longest that I saw Paul stayed in a place, but you can tell that it was done as the Lord led him to. What was he doing? He was proclaiming and teaching about Jesus Christ. There were many instances where you see Paul after preaching in one region, move immediately to another region. This explains to us that how long a mission lasts in a place is determined by God who has sends us.

It also explains what a missionary assignment is about viz: (1) Declaring the kingdom of God and teaching about the Lord Jesus Christ. (2) Proclaiming the kingdom of God which brings people in, by getting them saved and born again and teaching them, helps them grow and mature in Christ. A mission is as long as the Lord desires it to be. It can be short or long, however, at the end of the day what is most important is for the mission to be well accomplished and that it does not take longer or shorter than God wants it to be.

WHY FOREIGN MISSIONS?

This is indeed a big question- why do you have to travel thousands of miles away, when there are many souls around you that are dying and need the gospel? You must realise that where you go to preach is determined by where the souls God has called you to reach are, whether near or far.

For some of us, the souls that God has called us to reach are simply far away in other nations. If such stay around, struggling to gather people preach to, they may keep struggling to catch the attention of the people forever.

I once had a revelational dream where I saw myself ministering to a crowd in a hall. All the people in the first three roll were sleeping and an uninterested while the people from half the hall to the back seats were on fire and were touched by the anointing of the ministration. When I came back to myself, I immediately knew what it meant. I knew that my anointing is for people far away. The people near me get blessed but not like people far away. I know I am a missionary, an itinerary minister, and international global minister, I know the globe is my parish, while my local church is simply my home and base.

EARLY MISSIONARIES

The early missionaries launched out into missions and paid dearly as seeds for the global reawakening of the nations. I used the word re-awakening because the first awakening took place after the day of Pentecost through the first set of Apostles and missionaries. The early missionaries I am referring to are men and women like the missionaries that first arrived in England in 1837. Early missionaries traveled all the way to places they were forbidden to come; they risked their lives to go to places like China.

It is still illegal till now to go preach the gospel in China however, this has not stopped missionaries from risking their lives by going there as about 10,000 missionaries are in China currently. There are missionaries that died preaching the gospel e.g. Missionaries like Jim Elliot, Pete Fleming, Ed McCully, Nate Saint, and Roger Youde Rian. There were many more who suffered greatly for the sake of the gospel due to sicknesses, diseases. Many suffered from lack of adequate funding, and hostility from the people they went to reach out to.

Due to organizations that have been well established over a long period of time and have increased their root and have great financial power, there are ways in our days that many unnecessary sufferings are averted with adequate planning and funding. We cannot totally take away the risks, the challenges and suffering involved in missionary work, but it can be limited by being properly sent out and supported by Missionary organizations. I want to recommend to you watch a missionary based Christian movie titled "The forgotten ones". The movie was produced by The Mount Zion Christian Drama ministry.

MISSION BASE OR HEADQUATERS

Every foreign mission must and should have a home base where resources are being sent to them in the field. If there is a field, there should be a home base. Many missions suffer because though they go to foreign lands, they do not have a home base, where they are nourished and supported. They do not have a prayer covering from home. You see, every soldier deployed has a home base where they can recuperate. Going out without having a home base is reckless, so make sure you are sent out by God and authorities placed over you.

Act 1:1-3

1Now in the church at Antioch there were prophets and teachers: Barnabas, Simeon called Niger, Lucius of Cyrene, Manaen (who had been brought up with Herod the tetrarch), and Saul. 2While they were worshiping the Lord and fasting, the Holy

Spirit said, "Set apart for Me Barnabas and Saul for the work to which I have called them." 3And after they had fasted and prayed, they laid their hands on them and sent them off.

Remember it was from the church that Paul and Barnabas were sent out into the mission field as led by the Holy Spirit, through the authorities, by the laying on of hands. It is clear therefore, if you were not sent out through the church, the church will not be responsible for you.

RURAL MISSIONS

There is what we call the rural mission, this is the missionary work done and carried out in the rural areas around the world. Every nation has countryside or rural area and the city and towns. But many preachers or ministers in our days have their eyes on the city and high brow areas because nobody wants to risk the inconvenience of the rural areas.

However, the rural areas have their own peculiarities, which include the simple lifestyle of the villagers, humble heart, unique requirement for the demonstration of the power of God, great need for the application of faith because of needs that are obvious in the villages which are absent in the cities

It is my conviction that if the Lord is sending you on an assignment to the rural areas, He will put the passion on the inside of you for the rural areas and rural people. I for example enjoy going to stay and minister in the rural areas and being with the rural people than the city people. It is a feeling that is hard for me to explain and I do not know why I feel such joy in my heart. Even though I have been on apostolic missions to about 16 Nations across the globe, the best places I love to go are the rural parts of the nations. So, you can imagine, when others are impressed by the glamour of the city, I am drawn towards the rural areas. This is the passion that comes with the call.

During rural missions, there is a high tendency you experience a life of no electric power supply or inadequate power supply. This means you may not be able to keep your phone charged all the time. No electric power supply could also mean no internet or no strong internet connection. To thrive under such conditions requires you having a positive perspective and attitude and for me, I always see it as an opportunity to fast the internet and be more focused on God. It also gives me the opportunity to go organic or natural. It's a purging to my soul. It makes me focus on meditation on God instead of always being on social media.

PERSONAL IMPACT OF RURAL MISSIONS

In as much as rural missions avail us the opportunity to preach the word and bless souls at the same time, it has a great positive effect on our walk with God. Rural life during rural missions usually helps me appreciate God more for what I have in abundance which I have been taking for granted.

Fellowshipping with believers in the rural areas and getting to see how passionate they are for God, despite their level of standard of living also ministers to me personally just as their hunger for God touches and rubs on me. Trust me, seeing people without shoes dancing and praising God passionately on an uncemented floor will fire you up, especially if you are coming from developed nation.

A CALLED MISSIONARY

It is important that you do not just carry your bags and head to foreign missions, make sure you are called of God to be a missionary. How do you know that you are called to be a missionary? Let's find out below:

❖ VISIONS AND DREAMS

Paul an Apostolic missionary had an experience in the book of Act 16:9.

Act 16:9

9 During the night, Paul had a vision of a man of Macedonia standing and pleading with him, "Come over to Macedonia and help us." 10As soon as Paul had seen the vision, we got ready to leave for Macedonia, concluding that God had called us to preach the gospel to them....

Here, we can see that Apostle Paul had a calling to go to Macedonia through a night vision and at once he got ready to leave.

I remember a time in my life, I was in my twenties, and I had a night a vision also, and there an Angel said to me that Jesus our master is waiting for me on the field. At first, I did not fully grasp the meaning of "on the field" aspect of the vision until the Holy Spirit opened my understanding and I realized what he meant by "on the field", that it means the mission field.

I had seen myself in a dream being in a rural place in midst the of a family, ministering to them and praying for one of their daughters that was demon possessed and she was delivered, in the dream they offered their house for us to start a church. Wow!

God still speaks.

❖ INNER JOY, PEACE AND SATISFACTION

This is another way you will know if you are called to do this. The Joy and peace of God will guide you.

In the book of Act 16:17-18something happened there:

17 This girl followed Paul and the rest of us, shouting, "These men are servants of the Highest God, who are proclaiming to you the way of salvation!" 18 She continued this for many days. Eventually Paul grew so aggravated that he turned and said to the spirit, "In the name of Jesus Christ I command you to come out of her!" And the spirit left her at that very moment.

Here you can see that Paul lost his peace, because though the girl that was following them was saying the truth but not from a true spirit. She was speaking by the spirit of divination. Always check your inner peace and joy whenever you want to know if God is speaking or not. Though this can be a little bit tricky because sometimes people lose their peace simply because they are in the flesh concerning the situation and have not positioned themselves to hear from God, or their flesh is reacting to the will of the spirit. So, this method of following your inner peace and joy is for people who have completely surrendered their will and desires to God. It is for matured believers.

You see many times when I am about to leave home for the mission field, I miss my family seriously, though I know it is God's will for me to go to the field to serve the Lord, but immediately I get to the airport, a level of grace of God comes upon me and joy envelopes me right there. It is one of the ways God deals with me.

PREPARED TO BE A MISSIONARY

Just like any other kind of ministry, every missionary should have gotten a solid foundational Christian and biblical training. Missions are not for immature Christians because mission work involves leaving the known for the unknown. You must therefore be built up in faith, love, self-control, long suffering, peace, truth etc. If you look closely all the virtues listed here have something to do with the fruits of the Spirit.

Galatians 5:22-23;- But the fruit of the Spirit is love, joy, peace, forbearance, kindness, goodness, faithfulness, 23 gentleness and self-control. Against such things there is no law.

You need a lot of those to be able to do well in life talk less of on the mission field.

This does not mean that to be a missionary you have to be perfect, but you must be able and willing to let the Holy Spirit to help you to manifest the fruits. You must be yielded to the Holy Spirit. You must learn to count it all joy when you are faced with many trials,

James 1:2

Consider it pure joy, my brothers, when you encounter trials of many kinds, 3because you know that the testing of your faith develops perseverance....

A PEOPLE WITH A DIFFERENT BACKGROUND

As a missionary you will find yourself amidst people that are different from you in a thousand ways but you goal is to bridge that gap, in order to be able to reach them. Paul from his personal experience put it this way *"I have become all things to all people so the by all possible means I might save some".*

1 Corinthians 9:19

19 Though I am free of obligation to anyone, I make myself a slave to everyone, to win as many as possible. 20 To the Jews I became like a Jew, to win the Jews. To those under the law I became like one under the law (though I myself am not under the law), to win those under the law. 21 To those without the law I became like one without the law (though I am not outside the law of God but am under the law of Christ), to win those without the law.

...22 To the weak I became weak, to win the weak. I have become all things to all people so that by all possible means I might save some. 23 I do all this for the sake of the gospel, so that I may share in its blessings.

There was a time I was in a village on international missions in Tanzania, and people that were black skinned like me were amused by my way of dressing because I came from the US, though an African too. Some were laughing because people seem to mock what they regard to be odd, it required a level of maturity not to mind and to over look it. There were many times that I had to use a toilet system that I am not used to. It is always uncomfortable for me, in fact one of the uncomfortable moments in missions but I endure it.

2 Timothy 2:3:-Thou therefore endure hardness, as a good soldier of Jesus Christ.

To the people who hosted me, it is a normal way of life, but for the fact that we have different back grounds, it required endurance for me.

As a missionary you will have to be flexible and adaptable to different situations.

EAT WHATEVER IS SET BEFORE YOU

LUKE 10:7-9

7 Stay at the same house, eating and drinking whatever you are offered. For the worker is worthy of his wages. Do not move around from house to house. 8 If you enter a town and they welcome you, eat whatever is set before you.

Depending on the arrangement and circumstances surrounding your mission plans and trip, you may find yourself living in someone's home, as a missionary this is normal. This will involve eating from their table as a guest. As simple as this seems, it requires a lot of maturity and sometimes endurance and flexibility.

Not everyone finds it easy to eat food from a totally different culture, some cultures eat hot pepper while others don't. There have been many occasions I had running stomach eating food from other culture that I am not used to.

DIFFERENT WEATHER

Going outside you nation of birth or country where you were raised to a different nation as a missionary requires studying to know what kind of weather is over there. This will help you to know what kind of clothing you need to pack in your bags.

The first time I went on mission to Mexico, I went with all suits, shirts and ties. I didn't take time to know that is a warm region of South America. I suffered a lot of heat, and I was sweating profusely. By the grace of God, I have been going to Mexico for the past five years and now I know better. I travel there with light cloths. This has made mission much easier for me in that part of the world. If you are also going to Africa, I will advice you find out which part of Africa and know what to pack, same for Europe, America etc.

DIFFERENT EXPRESSIONS OF MISSIONS

Indeed, there are numerous expressions of missions assignment God can commit to a person and I like to share some of them with you:

❖ EVANGELICAL MISSION

This is the most common and traditional form of missions which involves going to new territories to take the message of salvation to a people who have never heard of Jesus before, start a church there and appoint pastors over them.

❖ MEDICAL MISSION

Medical mission is one of the expressions of Mission work which has to do with taking medical expertise to rural areas and places they do not have access to hospitals to touch lives with the love of Jesus through the gifted medical hands of Christian doctors and nurses. On such a mission, taking medications and administering it to the sick is a show of love that makes people's heart open to receive the message of Jesus and which can lead to the salvation of their souls. The unique thing about this is that people who would have never been able to have accessed to such medical attention because of lack of enough funds or distance from the city-based hospitals will be rescued because God sent His missionaries to their location. Love is the most powerful key that unlocks hearts and make them ready to accept Jesus as their Lord and saviour. There are many medical cases that do not require extra ordinary miracles only if the people are well informed on how to live a healthy lifestyle. Spreading the knowledge of living healthy lifestyle is one of the ways a medical missionary can help to save souls.

❖ EDCUATION-BASED MISSION

This is the kind of missionary work that is operated from the angle of spreading knowledge by trained teachers. When people are taught how to read and write, it gives them endless opportunities to be able to read the bible themselves and have access to the revelation of Jesus Christ since he devil thrives on ignorance. Teachers are destiny molders and role models and we need more teachers in the missionary work. What you know may look so common in the city, they may not even value it that much, but when you go to the missions in the rural areas with such skill and knowledge, the Lord will use it to turn hearts around for His glory.

❖ APOSTOLICAL MISSION

An Apostle is a voice and strength to the body of Christ, different from pastors set over a local assembly. An Apostle initiates, plants, starts, opens new channels and builds platforms for operations.

I have come to discover in my many years of traveling across the globe for Apostolic missions that there are many churches planted in the rural areas that are lacking and suffering from lack of adequate feeding of the people with the balanced diet of the word of God. Many pastors in the rural areas need encouragement, training and empowerment and this is a major work and burden of an Apostolic missionary which is not a title, rather, a great need. I was in a village in Uganda to train ministers on the platform of Liberty Global Academy and I was so touched when I saw the distance some pastors trekked to come for the training indicating that he need is real. There are many churches in the rural areas of the world that need an Apostolic covering and may not have enough money to bring guest ministers to help strengthen the work, but it is the job of the Apostolic missionaries to make themselves available and use their gifts, anointing, resources, knowledge and wealth of experience to build and strengthen the churches. Read below, one of Apostle Paul's letters to a church in Rome.

Romans 1:10

In my prayers at all times, asking that now at last by God's I will, I may succeed in coming to you. 11For I long to see you so that I may impart to you some spiritual gift to strengthen you.

A MISSIONARY MUST BE TRAINED

Many missionaries have gone out to the mission field by mere passion; however, passion without knowledge can burn and destroy. Therefore, a missionary must be trained on how to take care of their health. A missionary must be trained on how to relate with people of different languages (in fact should learn the language). A missionary must be trained on how to hear from God and be led by the Holy Spirit because a simple mistake can lead to a fatal end, hence, a missionary must be trained on basic life skills.

THE VISION AND THE MISSION

It is vision that births a mission and every mission must be given from above from the Lord Jesus Christ through the Holy Spirit via vision. Every mission cannot be the same, because our assignments differ and every genuine missionary must first be a true visionary who should be able to sayhat God commissioned him/her to do, say and state , where God has sent Him/Her and to whom God has sent you to carry out the assignment.

Considering the present situation of the world, anywhere can be a mission field not only in Africa, it can also be Europe or America however, without a clear-cut vision, every mission will look the same. I once saw a young man criticize a missionary because he was not doing missions according to the way the Europeans did it back then in Africa, in 1800 or

1900 because he failed to note that it is vision that determines mission.

A mission can be tailored depending on the vision or divine instruction towards education or health, feeding the hungry, or tailored towards security all of which are vehicles through which the gospel will penetrate the region.

One of the key visions our mission has is to liberate through teaching of the word and demonstration of power and the Holy Spirit. Our vision is to strengthen churches and believers, building them and helping them to live a relevant and victorious kingdom life on earth. We help build kingdom leaders through our academy (Liberty Global Academy).

A MISSIONARY MUST BE WILLING TO SACRIFICE THEIR COMFORT

Mission field is not the same as home, rather it is making a home of a foreign land and making families from a people different from you and to succeed at that, adaptation is the key here. You must find joy in living a life different from that which you are used to. It is an adventure. Sacrifice becomes easy when purpose is known and when the value of souls means everything to you as much as it means to God. The "Go" mission as Jesus gave it will require you drop the selfish and self-centered mentality. It will require from you, absolute trust in God. I have slept on a lot of beds and the rooms of strangers across the world. The fear of being attacked never bothered me because my trust has always being in the Lord. I have lived amongst brethren that I do not understand their language, so if they were planning against me, there was no way I could

know, but my trust has always being in the Lord
and I have always been peaceful, through it all.

THE HEART OF A GENUINE MISSIONARY

One key element must be at work for this to become a possibility and that is LOVE in capital letters. The most powerful driving force behind a missionary work is the love of God in the heart of an individual. You cannot be a racist and be able to bless people of a different skin color, tongue and culture.

A STORY OF AN EARLY MISSIOANRY - *Dr David Livingstone*

Livingstone went back to Linyanti but by the time he arrived his friend who was the chief had died. The new chief sekeletu wanted living stone to find the high ground but a woman asked him to come with her and introduced him to another chief in a new important place which is called Shinti , the chief accepted Livingstone and bonded with him. Not long after Livingston saw something they broke him, he saw for the first-time slave trade going on and he decided he will stop it.

A MISSIONARY MUST BE EQUIPED:

International mindset: international passport.

This involves getting your international passport and required visa needed. You must get information need.

A TRUE LIFE STORY OF A NATIVE OF GOMBA, A LADY I MET DURING ONE OF MY MISSIONS IN A VILLAGE IN UGANDA.

One a faithful day, myself and my team arrived Gomba , a village in Uganda. We were being hosted for the mission by a nomadic family who raises cows for a living. The man is a pastor and the wife a true Christian and a lover of God.

As we settled down and drank water given to us, the first thing that she said was, "This is a Christian Family", at first, I did not understand the full weight behind that statement. Not too long after that, she repeated that statement, which got me wondering why that was so important for her to say. She further went ahead to tell me her story.

She said, I married my husband at a very young teen age, and then my husband was three times this size. He could knock out a Bull; he was very strong and was also a very good wrestler. One day I had an experience that made me convert to Christianity – it was an encounter with Christ. I became a member of a church and became committed. When my husband heard about it, he was very angry but that did not change my faith, sometimes I will be refused food for days and be beaten, with rod used in driving cattle. Yet I kept praying for him, that he will also have an encounter with Jesus that will change his life. Being a young girl who had met with Jesus, I refused the ungodly acts and beliefs of my tradition and one of them is to allow my father-in-law have carnal knowledge of me. I refused him and that made my husband to be mad at me and he beat me till I was unconscious and refused me to come live in the house day and night, sunshine or rain fall. The persecution was much. I was so skinny that I could not walk well, yet I will walk on my feet miles upon miles to attend church services. My pastor kept encouraging me to pray for my husband and this went on for years. One day, he had a supernatural encounter with Jesus, and this melted him and transformed him completely, now he is a pastor and God has used him to build a lot of Church buildings for pastors and their congregation. This house was built by our first daughter and as you can see, we are blessed with four more. God has blessed us financially, and this is a Christian family.

This story really melted my heart and revealed to me that God has remnants and generals that may not be famous on earth but are highly honoured in heaven.

NOT IN VAIN

When the cost of being a missionary is counted it can be seen as a huge price to pay. It involves leaving loved ones and going into territories where you are not too certain if you will be accepted or not. It involves leaving behind our familiar and going into the unfamiliar. I remember my first mission trip to Ghana, there were times my host will not come early enough to take us to where we can get breakfast and we will have to stay hungry for hours. . There was a time someone confessed during one of our meetings after the power of God arrested her that she put poison in my food, so that I will not be able to come to minister that evening. There were times when our hosts will take money from us to book hotels and we will end up paying again because they did not pay as promised even after they had taken money from us, or instances where they promise to take care of our feeding and even raise offering for it in our presence and yet we were left to pay (what if we did not have enough money), this happened in Ghana, Tanzania and in Kenya, that is an example of what Paul the Apostle referred to as experienced with false brethren in *Galatians 2:4 And that because of false brethren unawares brought in, who came in privily to spy out our liberty which we have in Christ Jesus, that they might bring us into bondage:*

But I am here to tell you, that no matter what your own experience has been, it is not in vain. *Matthew 19:29 And everyone who has left houses or brothers or sisters or father or mother or wife or children or fields for the sake of My name will receive a hundredfold and will inherit eternal life.*

BEWARE OF FALSE EXPECTATIONS FROM THE PEOPLE YOU ARE GOING TO MEET.

In regions like East Africa, India or Pakistan, where the early European and American missionaries had gone with gifts and a lot of reliefs, including medical supplies, many of these people have developed a needy mentality. Whenever they hear that a missionary is coming from abroad, their expectations begin to rise and they begin to have false expectations. That is why Liberty Global Missions, which is the name of our missionary Christian organization does not go promising silver and gold but Jesus, salvation, healing and empowerment through knowledge of the word of God which is able to build the power and help them become independent on external supplies. We have received so many testimonies, people say they have never been this fed spiritually, that all those other missionaries come with are what they can eat for few days and their souls are left famished. I am not saying it is wrong to support the people with boreholes, schools etc. but if that is all that is provided then it has not fulfilled yet the great commission. Because of this, Pastors in a lot of the rural areas have taken advantage of foreign missionaries, charging them a lot of money to be able to be a blessing to the people.

BE STRATEGIC

Good and effective strategies are built around adequate knowledge. Since you have probably not been to the place of mission, majority of your knowledge should come through sound counseling and research.

Proverbs 11:14;Where no counsel is, the people fall: but in the multitude of counselors there is safety.

Mission is more fruitful and safer with good counsels. We are in the information age. The kind of knowledge that the early missionaries did not have access to, we have it. It is up to us to do our research and be humble enough to listen and take advice from good source.

However, lack of adequate strategy can lead to unwanted tragedy. I have heard of stories of missionaries who travelled out of their countries for mission without strategic plans. They went unprepared all in the name of loyalty to the call.

Also, get to know where you are going. Like I said, you can have access to knowledge by doing your research. Online has rich amount of information about almost everywhere on earth. (Daniel **12:4 But thou, O Daniel, shut up the words, and seal the book, even to the time of the end: many shall run to and from, and knowledge shall be increased).** Take advantage of the internet, it is not just for entertainment but building up, if you know how to use it.

Have a host who can speak their language and yours

Spy the land (everywhere Jesus went he sent his disciples ahead first)

Luke 10:1 After this the Lord appointed seventy-two others and sent them two by two ahead of him to every town and place where he was about to go. Even Jesus was strategic about his missions. It is important that we learn from this.

PRAY AND FAST

Going on a missionary trip is like going to another person's territory, It is important for you to pray and fast ahead.

Mark 3:27

In fact, no one can enter a strong man's house without first tying him up. Then he can plunder the strong man's house.

MISSIONS AND TECHNOLOGY

There is a great deal of advantage in technology that advances the effectiveness of Mission. There are mosquito repellents you can buy and keep in your bag. There are small sized battery running fans you can buy and pack along. There is plastic foldable mobile easy to pack toilet seats, to avoid discomfort in doing the number 2. You can as well pack snacks that will last long in your bag etc.

Technology has greatly influenced everything on this side of eternity including missions. During the early days of missions, there was no internet, no social media, there even was no plane, most people traveled through ship on the sea. Journeys that took a missionary month to accomplish now may take a missionary just an hour through flight. As a missionary, there are apps you can utilize to aid communication between you and people of a different language. I use one too. Depending on the side of the globe the mission is taking your to, if it is the tropic area of Africa, you might need a sunscreen, sunshade or shade hat. You will need to hydrate, therefore buy along good water bottle, mosquito net etc.

BODY ADAPTATION, SKIN ADAPTATION

IN 2019 I was in Kenya, in a village called Mawa in Eastern part of the continent of Africa for the mission. The weather was cold in the morning and very hot in the middle day. I started noticing my skin started peeling. At first, I was really concerned as it started spreading to my neck area and my arms. I started pealing it off and later after about one week, it started normalizing. I went with a special sunscreen lotion which I started applying to my skin which helped the healing of my skin to be faster.

DIGESTIVE SYSTEM

Eating food strange to your system may demand a need for adaptation your digestive system. Take along snacks, cocoa sachet powdered drinks. Take along simple and long-lasting snacks. The reason is that sometimes, they may come handy incase food is not easily accessible. Also,in caseyour digestive system is reacting to the food you ate, you need to know what you are allergic to in terms of food and avoid them e.g. if you are lactose intolerant and you travel to a place like East Africa where they drink fresh milk from cows and many other cow products like cheese.

JET LAGGING

Jet lag occurs due to difference in timing between where you are traveling from to you new location. It can range from 6 to 12 hours depending. This may make you feel like sleeping while everyone is awake and awake when everyone is sleeping in your new location which is the place of your missionary assignment. Don't be scared, it is not a spiritual attack, with time you will adapt to the local timing of your new location. Apart from all these, there are other things your body might have to adjust to, due to different unique nature of every individual.

TRAVELING FOR MISSION

To travel for international mission, you may have to join an already established Christian missionary body. Also, you can travel by yourself, if you have a Christian body of good reputation that you can trust in the nation of your missionary assignment and they invite you over. However, do not go without adequate and necessary arrangement. I have heard of individuals who were invited by someone or a group of people over for mission, only for the person invited to arrive at the country of destination at the airport and not find the host or anyone representing the host and they were stranded. Make sure a solid and trustworthy arrangement has been made for you.

WARNING!

Do not travel based on assumption, thinking you can fend for yourself. There are many things about where you are going that are totally different from where you are going. Especially if you are going for the first time, make sure you are well covered.

GET YOUR INTERNATIONAL PASSPORT

If your missionary assignment is outside your country of residence, you cannot travel without a valid passport.

OBTAIN YOUR VISA

If your place of mission assignment is outside the country of your residence make sure you apply for your visa ahead of time. Depending on the passport of the nation you have, you may not need to apply for visa, and you might need to so. Do your research and find out if you will be needing a visa or not. For some countries they will offer you visa on arrival. All in all, please do your findings.

MISSION IN DANGEROUS AREAS

There have been cases where the missionary work is being carried out in dangerous areas of the world, especially places where preaching the gospel has been formally declared as illegal. There are also places where there is insecurity and traveling there is highly insecure due to religious intolerance. These are regions where missionaries are being kidnapped and killed. Anywhere you want to go, it is important that you do your research and count the cost and not be ignorant, as this will enable you to pray and plan adequately and apply wisdom for high productivity.

MY LIFE AND MISSIONARY JOURNEY

I received a call into the ministry from the age of thirteen. I had a dream to join the Navy, but God had a different plan for me. I finally started the journey of this ministry at the age of 19. The Lord showed me in between different visions where I saw myself in different continents of the world as an Apostolic Missionary. I had seen myself in places like India, Africa, Europe and America. The journey for me did not start out by my traveling out of the country of my birth (Nigeria). My journey started out though called to preach, the Lord instructed me to join a gospel musical group. It was the place I started my ministerial experience, within the group we usually had camp meetings where we fast and pray for days. I learnt humility, diligence and long suffering in this ministry. Today I am grateful the Lord allowed me to pass through the musical group because till now, the gift of music helps me to stir the atmosphere wherever I find myself before I preach, teach and flow in power gift for healing and miracles.

God opened doors for me to travel from state to state within Nigeria and I made sure I stayed faithful to the call of God. Apostolically, my operations were within states in Nigeria. Sometimes it involved the danger of night, sleeping in abandoned cars, there were times when I travel from one end of the country to another for missions and the public transport hired will refuse to go further when it is dark and ask everyone to come down at the middle of the highway and ask us all to go look for where to sleep because of the fear of the danger and armed robbers. However, the Lord has kept me through it all.

The Lord called me into full time ministry and that for me, meant people(Family members), calling me unreasonable many wondered if I would have a future, I suffered hunger and a lot of lack in those days, but I remained faithful to the call. Gradually people that saw the impact of the missions started giving towards the mission and God sustained us and the ministry. The mission operated through different avenues, music, creative art, preaching, healing etc. God reached souls in their thousands.

In 2007, the Lord said the time for my international missions has come. I did not know how it would happen. I did not know how to get a visa; I did not even know if it was a visa I get first or an international passport or a ticket. The Lord connected me to my wife and helper in the ministry and we got married in 2007. The mission right from 2006 reached Ilorin, Kwara State in thousands of souls, based on a vision the Lord showed me - in the vision, I was on a stage where different people were expressing worship to God through different African artistic expressions, I discussed it with my partner in ministry then and we ran with the vision called

Ijinle worship festival. Many souls were reached. In 2008, all hell broke loose, the government was ill informed about the intention and the vision of the outreach, though it was obviously stated in our brochures. The police were released to stop people from coming out for the gathering, yet people pushed, it became a movement that people were willing to die for and eventually hosted the outreach festival. In 2009, the Lord instructed me that it is time for my ministry to move to the US, then opened the way for me and my family settled in New York where we have been operating from to the whole world since 2010. I became a missionary not only to America but to the world because my American passport became a tool the Lord gave me to travel the world and preach the gospel.

Right here in New York, the mission has planted her headquarters in Syracuse, and centers in Ghana, Nigeria and South Africa. The mission has traveled to about 16 Nations across the globe such as Mexico, Canada and other states in the U.S, Nigeria, Ghana, New Zealand, Pakistan, South Africa, Uganda, Kenya, Tanzania, Rwanda, UAE, etc

IS MISSION FOR EVERYBODY?

Is mission for everybody? My answer is yes but not every aspect of mission is for everyone because mission is wide and deep. The scriptural origin of mission is from these scriptures which came from the mouth of our Lord Jesus Christ and savior.

Mark 16:15

And He said to them, "Go into all the world and preach the gospel to every creature.

Matthew 28:19

Therefore, go and make disciples of all nations, baptizing them in the name of the Father, and of the Son, and of the Holy Spirit,

Our Lord Jesus Himself was the first missionary who left His glory and comfort in heaven and came to this sinful world as a human with the mission to rescue humanity from the clutches of the devil which is sin and death. After His death and resurrection, He still made sure He presented Himself to the disciples with proofs for forty days, teaching them about the Kingdom of God.

Act 1:2

Until the day He was taken up to heaven, after giving instructions through the Holy Spirit to the apostles He had chosen. 3After His suffering, He presented Himself to them with many convincing proofs that He was alive.

He appeared to them over a span of forty days and spoke about the kingdom of God and so Jesus did not command us to do what He has not done. Everything Jesus asked us to do, He led us to do them by example.

Now, back to the question "is mission for everyone, my answer again is "yes". We have been commanded by our Lord to go to the world and preach the gospel, but we must know that our assignments differ from one another. Not everyone has been called to go to foreign missions, not everyone has been sent to leave their jobs and go full time to missions. Some fulfill the mission in the place of their job, business, and city where they are based. Jesus appeared to Paul telling him not to be afraid of speaking about the gospel in the new mission territory because He has many of His people in that city. Imagine if Jesus did not have anyone in the city because they have all gone on foreign mission, who will host Paul and create avenue and platform to preach the gospel safely in that city?

Act 18:9

One night the Lord spoke to Paul in a vision: "Do not be afraid; keep on speaking; do not be silent. 10For I am with you, and no one will lay a hand on you, because I have many people in this city."

There are many nations I have been able to go on mission because God has planted indigenous missionaries who were native of the land there to host me and make the work easier. So not everyone is called to go, some are called to stay but still with the mindset of a missionary. We must be aware that as much as there are lost souls thousands of miles away, there also lost souls in our neighborhood, therefore missions can still be fulfilled a stone throw away from us. Foreign mission should be a response to God's calling either through a strong inner impression of the Holy Spirit or visions or dreams or any other way God leads an individual.

KINGDOM MISSION SPONSORS

In the previous chapter, we dealt with the topic of whether mission is for everyone or not and my answer was "yes" mission is for everyone but in different ways. Not everyone will be called to travel for missions, not everyone will be called out of their professional jobs to go for foreign missions, but some will be called to use their finance to fund the gospel, their money can get to where they can't go physically to help enhance the gospel.

Luke 8: 1-3

Among them were Mary Magdalene, from whom he had cast out seven demons, Joanna, the wife of Chuza, Herod's business manager, Susanna, and many others who were contributing their own resources to support Jesus and his disciples.

From the scripture above you can see, that there were many who continuously contributed to the sponsorship of the Jesus' mission on earth. This has been the foundation of the operation of mission, and it will continue to be. These sponsors were not the one preaching or healing the sick, but their resources helped as a vehicle to make it happen. Some people are in this category of missions.

MISSION IN CHINA DURING THE PANDEMIC

China is one of the most anti-gospel nations on the earth that literarily resist the gospel mission, such that the churches in China only operate secretly, underground. During the covid-19 pandemic, when China was really one of the hot spots of Covid 19, Bibles were being allowed to be shipped in and the gospel was allowed to be preached. Missionaries recognize the truth that the darker it gets the greater opportunity it is for light to shine even brighter. Yes, it is more challenging to travel to foreign countries for missions during the pandemic, but it is still possible. Personally, I have been to about four different Nations to preach the gospel during the pandcmic. One of the challenges is that you have to keep doing the covid tests, when I went to South Africa and Uganda,(South and East Africa) I had about four different covid tests, without the tests you won't be able to fly in or out of the countries, so that has come to become part of the life of a traveling missionary.

FAITH VERSUS RISK

The element of faith cannot be ruled out in missions. It has been the case right from the very inception of gospel mission till now and looking at mission from a natural point of view; you will see risks more than any other things. For some, even the thought of getting into the plane to fly gives them a feeling of risk. To others, going to a foreign land, to be with a people they do not understand their language gives them a feeling of risk. One of my close friends once expressed his fear when it comes to going to live in the same house with complete strangers. Considering all these forms of risks not to talk about the risk of health, security etc.as a missionary, some even go to places where it is known for hostility towards the gospel and preachers. Considering all these risks, the only way you can bypass all those and go and preach the gospel at this capacity is by faith in God, faith in Jesus as your sender, faith in the presence of the Holy Spirit and faith in the promises of God.

I have been to many nations facing the risk of covid 19, When I go to preach, they hug me, I lay hands on them to minister healing etc., yet I have never for once tested positive of covid 19. My faith is in Jesus who has sent me. The Lord has been my protector, provider, peace, joy and success.

PICTURES

Liberty Global Mission to Dubai.

Liberty Global Mission to Uganda.

MISSION AND THE POWER OF THE HOLY SPIRIT

Mission has largely been characterized with building schools, hospitals, orphanages etc. This is superb, but as wonderful as it is something has been largely missing in a lot of mission works except for some few ministries and that is the power of the Holy Spirit at work, healing, miracles, signs and wonders, deliverances etc Jesus said to His disciples in the book of Luke 24 verse 49" ***And behold, I am sending the promise of My Father upon you. But remain in the city until you have been clothed with power from on high.***"

Jesus practically told them, do not go until you are clothed with power from on high. This means missions will be impossible without the power of the Holy Spirit.

Nothing gives me greater joy than when I see Souls won to the kingdom of God, when I see the

Healing meeting in Canada.

sick healed, oppressed delivered and people getting filled by the Holy Spirit. Jesus said to His disciples as He sent them on the kingdom mission in *Matthew 10:8 As you go, preach this message: 'The kingdom of heaven is near.' 8Heal the sick, raise the dead, cleanse the lepers, drive out demons. Freely you have received; freely give.*

In January 2022, I was on a mission to UAE, on a Sunday morning service (the historical first Sunday service allowed in United Arabian Emirate), I was led by the Holy Spirit to pray for people's finances (due to financial hardship caused by the covid 19 pandemic), a woman came out to be prayed for, and suddenly she told me that she came to be prayed for because she had brain cancer that had spread, by the grace of God and faith in the name of Jesus, I laid hands on her and prayed for her healing, a Sunday after which I had left UAE, she came back to the church to testify how she had gone for a medical checkup and the cancer had disappeared.

Woman healed of cancer by the power of the
Holy Spirit, by Christ stripes and to the Glory of
God.

DEMONS CAST OUT WERE SURPRISED

In a particular village Kiyongoga in Uganda, during one of our missions there, there was a boy that was possessed by demons. The boy was raised by a single mom; the father had left him and the mom. The father of the boy was in a cult and shared the same demon with the boy which made life difficult for the boy. The people had tried all they could, yet the boy was not delivered. During one of the missions meeting in the evening, I prayed for the boy by the grace of God, the power of the Holy Spirit came upon the boy, and the demon in him started manifesting, throwing the boy here and there, and the demon in the boy started to speak through the boy in the Luganda language, asking in a surprising manner saying "you mean you bought your ticket and flew all the way from America to cast me out?" That was the last thing the demon said before it flew out of the boy and the boy has been free ever since to the Glory of God.

Now that got me thinking, that even the demon in the remote places settles there believing no body will care enough to come and set the captives free. Mostly the reason it is so, is because many of the churches there are not buoyant financially enough to invite matured ministers from afar, to minister to them or train them. It takes a minister with the heart of a missionary to use his or her own money to travel that far with no strings attached.

LITTLE BOY HEALED OF STRANGE SKIN DISEASE

Mission to Kenya was awesome, there was a great move of the Holy Spirit. God established new kingdom relationships. One of such was with a young family of a pastor in Kenya. Few weeks after I arrived back in the United States, The young pastor called me over the video call and told me of what was really bothering his family, His little son had developed a swollen skin and they did not know what to do, he asked me to pray over the phone and lo and behold after the prayer, he called me the following day of how the power of God came upon the boy and the swollen skin went back to normal. The boy was healed instantly. Glory to God!

JEHOVAH ELOHIM

I was in Uganda in 2019 on a mission and suddenly I received a call from a Ugandan friend of mine who is based in the US. He expressed his desire for me to visit his ministry in a village in Uganda, spoke with my mission coordinator in Uganda, when we were just coming from another ministration and I was really physically tired, but I agreed to visit his ministry. Off we drove and it was almost five hours drive into the thick jungle of Uganda, when we arrived, we were received by the ministry coordinators there.

I was ushered into the place where I was to minister, the place was a dry and dusty ground, the children were without shoes, the building was made of aluminum sheet, no blocks, no bricks. The rest of the land had no buildings, just bare. There was no microphone, no speakers, no drums, no keyboard. Already my voice was already gone from the previous ministration. As I opened my mouth to minister, I heard the Holy Spirit instructing me to speak about the "God the Creator" Jehovah Elohim from the book of Genesis chapter 1 from verse 1. As I began, the hand of the Lord came strongly upon me to prophecy. I started making prophetic declarations that there shall be clinics here, I see hostels here, I see dining here, I see library here etc. It was all recorded by the ministers there. About a year later, the leader of that ministry sent me pictures of the place, with pictures of clinic, library, hostels etc just as prophesied.

MY FIRST MISSIONARY EXPERIENCE IN UAE

Someone who had worked with me as a missionary to East Africa, Uganda to be precise, called me and told me about the need to reach UAE with the gospel. I prayed about it and felt a release in my heart to move with it. I prepared, bought my ticket and his own ticket too and we were set to go. I had a lot of fears to conquer in my heart; UAE is an Islamic nation consisting of kingdoms. I have never been there before; I knew nobody there except the person that works with me who is inviting me. I overcame the doubts, and I was in the plane, flying all the way to the Middle East to preach the gospel. When we arrived at the airport, I was picked up by a nice Christian brother and was taken to where I would be lodging. To my surprise, the room was full of bunk beds. A lot of brothers were in the room, they were Pakistani brothers. Some were able to converse with me in English, but some were not able to. They received me with Christ's love but still wondering why I came all the way.

The brother who invited me told me that they were friends and they have known each other for a long time. Until later when I got to know that they only met on Facebook. I was shocked and I started asking him why he lied to me and brought me into such risk. When the leader of the brother saw the way, I openly rebuked him, he had the courage to open up to me, saying "man of God. When you arrived, we went to search for you on YouTube and we saw a lot of your messages and realized you a genuine man of God. Why did you allow this brother to deceive you? They warmed up to me, fed me and I learnt a bit of their culture, they became extremely nice to me. After three days and there was no sure place that we could preach, UAE is strict with laws regarding preaching, I stared praying that God would not allow me to go there in vain, but that he will open to me an effective door of ministry. On Friday morning, I was woken up, that there is a pastor who was willing to have me come and preach in their church, that was nothing but God at work. I dressed up and off we went. God showed up in His power, healing deliverances broke out and salvation of Souls. Since that day, the Lord established a close relationship between my family and the family of the pastor of the church. I have revisited the ministry over there to bless the people of Pakistan for five years consecutively. Hallelujah. The path sometimes may be rough, but If God is the one leading you, the doors will open for you.

MY EXPERIENCE IN TANZANIA (BEWARE OF FALSE BRETHREN)

My mission to Rwanda came with a price. After we arrived in Rwanda and were welcomed in by our host, He was very kind to tell us to feel free to eat anything we were given by the hotel. We knew why we were there was not for pleasure, we were as modest as possible. We ministered to the people's needs as much as it was within our spiritual and physical capacity. Souls were won for Christ and lives were blessed. One thing that I sensed in the spirit was that though they had a pastor, they were under a heavy burden and chains of limitations. At first, I did not know why but not too long after I discovered it was because the very one that was supposed to show them the way out was the very one holding them down in their bondage. After ministering to them, we saw the pastor always coming out to raise money, telling the congregation that the money was for the feeding of the guest ministers (us), which was very unnecessary because we were ok. The whole secret came out the day were to leave Tanzania and the pastor instructed the hotel administrator to take from us all the amount of money that covers the cost for our feeding from us (despite the fact that he took the money from the church members) and he had told us that he would pay for it. We were shocked but not ashamed, I brought my wallet out and paid and we left.

The question is what if we did not have enough money to pay? It would have become a scandal ***"Missionaries from US held down for eating and not paying the hotel".***

The lesson here is, make sure you travel with adequate resources, do not be a nuisance. Do not go by the words of anyone, be prepared. I have heard of people abandoned by their host at the airport of mission. Make sure you allow the Holy Spirit to lead you. Do not assume every Christian brother or sister showing interest to host your missionary mission is genuine. Pray and prepare well.

WHAT KIND OF MISSIONARY ARE YOU?

This question thrown at you will suggest that there are different kinds of missionaries. Like I said earlier in this book, your mission is determined by your vision. Your vision should be determined by the unique assignment that God has for you as a missionary.

There are missionaries that God will ask to leave their place of birth and go to a different location and stay there all the days of their lives. This is the traditional missionary, there were white Europeans or Americans that traveled to Africa as missionaries and stayed there, planted schools and hospitals. I attended one of such schools planted by missions both in my primary school and secondary school. In such schools, Christian values are taught alongside secular education. One way or the other this helped form my early days foundation as a person and as a Christian.

We grew up seeing white missionaries around us in school. Their lives were sowed out to the mission work. There is a youth camp in a place called Eyenkorin at the outskirt of Ilorin, Kwara State Nigeria, this camp is a Christian camp planted by a white missionary by the name Mama Kathryn M. Dick.

A major part of the formation of my Christian life as a youth was formed by camp meetings organized on this campground. Prophecies that shapened my life and ministry today were released on this campground though I can't say if I ever met Mama Kathryn before she slept in the Lord.

Her vision which found expression in her mission was towards the youth in a region of Nigeria. A place far away from her native land. As missionaries, we need to be aware that our assignment as missionaries must be well received from the Lord and not be as a result of copying what we see others doing. Thank God for Mama Kathryn for yielding to the Lord.

AVOID NEGATIVE STEREOTYPES

Have you ever heard negative stereotypical statements about a race, country or continent? These kind of statements can cause fear in your heart and make one lose the enthusiasm to want to go to the land God is sending one. I grew up watching movies about the one-time president of Uganda by the name Idi Amin and according to the movie, he was a man that struck terror in the heart of the people. When I received an invitation to go to Uganda for the mission, I was at first skeptical about going but praise God I was able to overcome the fear. Uganda has been a mission field for me for over four years. I have built strong kingdom relationships and the people are lovely people. Overcoming the fear created by negative stories about a nation you are sent to, is a big huddle to cross.

Till today I am always grateful to God that I had gone to Mexico for missions and had experienced the warmth of Mexican families in mission before I started hearing about the stereotypes about them. I have been going to Mexico for missions for a period of five years now. Do not be led by fear but be led by the spirit of God. Your destiny is at the other side of your fear.

AS A MISSIONARY YOU MUST BE MATURED IN YOUR CHARACTER

The first aspect of your mission as a missionary is to relate with people. Before you open your mouth to speak the first word, they are watching your character. They want to know who you are. You are a kingdom diplomat; you are a kingdom representative. You are not representing your country, you are not representing your natural tribe, you are representing God's kingdom. The fruits of the spirit must find full expression in you. Missionary work is for the matured in the spirit.

A BRIEF ABOUT ME

My name is Omodunni David Dada. I was born on the 10th of October in 1975 to the family of Titus Ekundayo and Esther Olanireti Dada. I am third of six siblings. I was born in Zaria, Kaduna state, in the northern part of Nigeria.

When I was four years old, my family moved from Zaria to Ilorin, Kwara state in Nigeria. My Dad was a trained civil engineer. He trained in Nigeria and in India. He decided to move to Ilorin in other to start his private building contractor business. I grew up in the city of Ilorin. My mom was a trained teacher, sometimes she will have to leave me with my aunty to baby sit me. I loved my mom very much, separating from her for few hours was like forever as a child. Later when I was old enough to start school, I started attending Chapel Nursery and primary school, same school as my other older siblings. Primary school was fun and at the same time a lot of discipline. This formed a very strong foundation of my life; I can still remember my primary school friends that I consider to be my brothers and sisters.

Part of my childhood days can still be remembered for Christmas and Easter celebrations when our parents will buy for us Christmas and Easter cloth and shoes and visiting the village where my dad grew up from to visit our grandparents. I can remember a day, some uniformed men came with my uncle to Ilorin, and my uncle was in the Nigeria navy, I was a little boy about 10 years of age. I asked my mom, who the uniform men were, and she told me they were Navy boys. I told my uncle I'd loved to join the Navy and since them my dream to join the Navy became unquenchable. At age 13, I was sick and admitted in the hospital for four weeks. While laying the sick bed, a man walked straight into my hospital room and asked whose son is this? My mom said mine, and the man said, "*This boy is not an ordinary boy, he is a mighty man of God*" God is going to use this boy mightily in the ministry. I did not want to hear those words, because I had already made up my mind to be in the military when I grow up. Few weeks later, I was strong and had recovered from typhoid fever. It was as if the words the prophet released at the hospital was a key that unlocked revelations, because since then I started having visions upon visions about my ministry and calling. Be aware that I was only 13 years of age at junior high school, the same year that I got born again and got baptized under the pastoral leadership of Pastor Emmanuel Oshe at Living Faith Church now known as Winners Chapel International. In 1988. I accepted the call to the ministry when the Lord spoke to me in a vision, I was in the company of four friends, and I saw three people approaching in the night covered with skin disease, and I heard the Lord said to me, "if you separate yourself unto me, you will lay your hands on the sick and they shall be healed. I said "Lord I want to serve you but I do not want to end up (name undisclosed for good reasons) like a particular man of God who fell into sin of immorality and was ashamed due to scandal, but I discovered the Lord expected me to trust Him to keep me from falling , so I separated myself in obedience and laid my hands on the sick and they were healed instantly" when I gained consciousness, it was my acceptance to the call of the ministry that the Lord had called me into. Life continued as a young boy, I attended Mount Carmel College, a Catholic mission secondary school for six years and graduated.

THE STRUGGLE BEGAN

After my senior secondary school examination and UTME that is needed for me to gain admission to the university, I lost my best friend in 1993. We had been friends since primary school and we lived in the same Estate. We were so close that, we were closer than my blood brother. He traveled and never came back; it was a blow on me. I felt so miserable that I felt ill, his name was Baba Tunde. After the incidence my dad suggested that I go visit my cousins in Lagos, to be able to get things off my mind.

When I was in Lagos, one evening, I was about to step into the bathtub and I heard an audible voice clearly in my native language "o ni lo school. Sugbon ma toju e" meaning "You are not to further your formal education, but I will take good care of you" I knew it was the Lord, but who do I tell this to and my heart was beating fast yet I had a kind of peace that surpassed my understanding. It was mixture of both, when was due to my head reasoning the other was my spirit man. I acted as if I heard nothing; I went on with my life. When I Left Lagos for Ilorin, I went straight ahead to retake my senior secondary school certificate exam because I did not perform excellently the first time but this time I came out with good grades. I went ahead against the instruction I heard and applied to a college of Agriculture in Akure, Ondo State, Nigeria and I was picked instantly, my dream aside joining the military was to have a big animal farm, to sustain myself when I begin ministry full time this was in 1995. My period in college was one of the toughest periods of my life, the finance was not there, hunger tormented me in school, there were times as a student that I won't have what to eat for three days, yet I would attend classes and go through the rigor of agriculture, cultivating etc.

After college days in Akure, I started developing heavy chest pain, and I knew I had to obey the call to full time ministry and the school of the spirit. I said to the Lord to heal me and I will comply with His demands, and He did but that was just the beginning of the life training. God instructed me to join a gospel musical group that had been asking me to join their group for a while and I had been turning them down, because my calling was not musical, really? Yes really? Lord, are you asking me to go these routes? The Lord showed me in a vision, that the group is a vehicle that will take me to a junction where I will branch and take the direction; He wants me to go, so I obeyed the Lord and joined. My first experience of ministry began. This musical group was not just any kind of group, we would be asked to fast, pray in the spirit and share the word, go for camping and all manna of spiritual exercises. This season of my life, a lot of people got to know me as a gospel singer but had no idea about the covenant and calling of God concerning my life in the direction of Apostolic, missions, church planting, writing, healing etc After a while in this direction, I had another vision.

I saw myself singing and prophesying and laying hands on people and the spirit of the Lord started moving with healing, signs and wonders. I knew it was time to move in a different direction. This was around year 2000. In 2001, I was appointed to lead this Gospel music group after several prestigious and anointed leaders had passed the baton. When it got to my turn to lead, unlike other leaders that were splitting songs into parts, organizing concerts and teaching songs, I was doing anointed impartations, teaching and stirring the members for future revivals. Sometimes we could have all night Holy Ghost night. I only led the group in Ilorin for a year and from there I was in Lagos for a recording of my project and worked with a church called Light

House Church as a pastor in charge of worship (though I knew, this was not my calling), whenever I stood to minister, the power of God will hit the place and everyone would be under the power of the Holy Spirit, it was never what I planned but the fire could not be contained or restrained, the pastor started complaining and in his own words, he said I was too spiritual. I was faced with an option to either tone it down or leave.

MY JOURNEY AND MY TIME IN ABUJA AND JOS NIGERIA

I left Lagos with the intention to go to Jos Plateau State Nigeria for my recording project. The time I left coincided with the moment I was ready to continue my recording project in Jos at Dr Panaam's studio. I packed my bags and left for Jos, on my way to Jos I stopped over to spend a night in Abuja with my brother and friend , who was the head of music department in an RCCG branch in Abuja, he persuaded me to minister that same night, I reluctantly agreed but again the Holy Spirit hit the place with His presence and power , everyone were on the floor crying and drunk in the spirit. On our way home that night the Pastor asked me some deep questions "who are you, where are you coming from and where are you going? I tried as much as possible to answer the question to the best of my understanding. The Pastor persuaded me to stay in Abuja while I do my recording in Jos. I agreed (though I never sought the face of the Lord about this). My period in Abuja was an interesting period. I was not paid a salary, but whenever I had a need the pastor tries his best to help. People in the church started giving me dollars in envelops because they were getting imparted by my ministrations. I liked it but one day I had a vision and the Lord said to me "go back to Ilorin until I launch you out by myself"

BACK IN ILORIN IN OBEDIENCE TO DIVINE ORDER

Immediately after the order given to me to go back to Ilorin, I packed my bags and left for Ilorin. People thought I was crazy, who does that? But I knew obedience to God is the only way to fulfill the purpose He has for my life. This was in 2003. All through 2003, I sought the face of the Lord concerning what to do. By now, I had no brother or sister around in Ilorin, I had no friends. All I had was God. I had no choice than to spend time with God. This was the period I built my spiritual life to a higher dimension.

In year 2004, the Lord said it is time to start out my ministry formally and take the fire around, so we started "God's Spring Konnect Africa" Though still using the vehicle music, but the prophetic move, healing and deliverance and Apostolic move was birthed, and we were moving from church-to-church within Ilorin city in Nigeria with fire. Soon that same year 2004, I was invited to Abuja by Baptist Church for a five-day revival. I taught on intimacy with God and moved in the Holy Spirit demonstration and power, there was massive healing and the Reverend of the church who had never spoken in tongues before was filled with the Holy Spirit with the evidence of speaking in tongues. This move continued till 2005. Now other states in Nigeria started hosted us and started receiving the same impact. In 2005/early 2006 the Lord showed me in a vision, a massive outreach which rode on the vehicle of creative art, music, dance, poetry, stage drama, it was a form of Christian festival of some sought and it was so huge that when I gained consciousness, I was asking God how this would be. This was the period a young man came looking for me, seeking that I mentor him in the area of recording his musical album. We grew so close that his parents, brothers and sisters became family to me. Then we formed a Christian organization called GM (Generation Worship) He had a desire to organize concerts which we agreed to push through GM, but I presented the Vision God gave me, which was the Festival, I named it Ijinle worship Festival: so, we decided to push Ijinle worship festival first, Just as God showed me, ijinle worship festival blew up all across the city, this was in July 2006. The success was so huge that we focused our attention on Ijinle. My Dad attended ijinle and said "I have never attended any program as huge as this in my life"

Prior to this time, My Dad Engr T.E Dada, thought I wanted to be in the ministry because I was lazy, I actually said it but his opinion changed when he saw the commitment and work that went into organizing the mega worship festival that drew people in their thousands, almost ten thousand people, within and outside

the venue. Ijinle worship festival was organized
and held in 2006 2007, 2008.

I LOST MY DAD

The latter part of my dad's life was when we were closest. All my siblings had left Ilorin. My mom had separated from my dad. I would have left too to start my own life, but God said I should return to Ilorin in an estate called Adewole Estate, which I obeyed. I did not know why God gave me that instruction until later. This was the period my dad and I would sit and really talk. This was the period he instilled some important values in me. One word I can never forget he said to me was from *Ecclesiastes 12:1 Remember your Creator in the days of your youth, before the days of trouble come and the years approach when you will say, "I find no pleasure in them.* This scripture and word he said to me, guided my life and it is still doing so till now. I believed this is what he would do if he had another chance to relieve his life. I saw my life as an opportunity to do it right early in life in order to end well at old age.

At a point I felt frustrated still living in my father's house in my mid-twenties, but the Lord said, He will launch me out by himself. So, I focused on the work the Lord placed in my hands and one morning the Holy Spirit instructed me to go round the compound and look around, if possible, take some pictures because He is about to launch me out and I will not be able to come back there even if I wanted to. So, I obeyed God. Not too long after that, my dad, decided to sell that house and I moved to my own apartment, and he moved on to his new house. Now the house has been sold and the word of the Lord came through because there was no way I could go back to that house that I lived in as a little boy till mid-twenties.

Following God's instructions sometimes may make you look stupid and slow. It was hard for people to understand me. No lady wants to believe in such a guy to want to marry him.

Talking about ladies, I tried a couple of relationships and some were nothing but distractions. I was in a relationship where the lady believed all I could contribute was spiritual because she believed in the anointing in my life but never agreed with me concerning any decisions on the level of reasoning or intellect (imagine being seen as spiritual but unintelligent) It led to arguments and sometimes started seeing tendencies in her to be physically aggressive , at this point I knew there was no future in that relationship because I did not want a marriage that I will have to get into physical combat with my own wife. All those were around 2005 and I experienced multiple heartbreaks which were very emotionally tough for me, as a young minister. I wanted to love and be loved badly, that I went from one relationship to the other. After that relationship, I wanted to get married so bad that I went into another relationship, with a lady I met in church (I used to think all church girls were good girls). In this relationship, I discovered I was drained, she demanded I sell all my properties to meet her needs, I was ministering but I was dying. We agreed to get married. You see I am a committed lover, I have never double dated in my life, if I am in, I am in, that is how God made me, so she took advantage of it, called off our relationship few weeks to our family introduction that we had sewed cloths and spent money to plan. This broke me so bad, but this was the very time we started preparation for Ijinle worship festival, and my partner in ministry came into my life Dr Jerry K. The Lord used him, his parents and siblings to fill the void in my heart; I found a family in them. Instead of sinking into depression I concentrated all my energy and emotions into organizing ijinle. We leave home in the morning and work till late in the night. From studio cooking jingles for the event, to radio and television stations for promotions. Sometimes in the taxis, sometimes on foot, sometimes in the rain, sometimes in the sun. We were consumed by the passion and driven by the vision. Finally, the day for the first ijinle came and the whole city was on fire for God. My dad attended and said this words that gave me joy till this day, "I used to think you were lazy but I discovered when a man finds what he loves doing, he is the most diligent man in the world" He saw the level of commitment that went into it and he saw the result. My dad said "I have never attended a meeting with this size of crowd and impact in a place before"

Few months towards the end of 2006 my dad fell ill, I was the only one around to take care of him, stayed in the hospital with him. All other siblings were too busy to come pay him a visit except his first born who came once and after that only came when he heard that he had died to prepare for his burial. It was tough, but God helped me. People only knew the ministry side of my life but only few friends knew what I was going through. God sent some few friends into my life to bear the burden with me. Moving my dad's property from the old house which he sold to the new house which he newly bought, alone with a friend, I will never forget her, Jenny (not her real name). No sibling cared enough to come around, why? they were busy. I remember the night my dad was about to pass on to glory, he asked for his first born but he was not there. I wanted to hold his spirit, so he won't die, but then I heard the Lord says "let him go" he needs to rest. The Lord said "He has lived his life, now you live yours" I can never forget this life changing moments and statements. At that moment I felt like God was telling me, that blow it.

SHE WANTED LOVE AND SEX BUT DID NOT WANT TO GET MARRIED

Jenny (not her real name) had become my good friend after I moved into my own apartment, I met her in the new neighborhood, her singing voice drew me close to her. The first time I had her sing, she was washing outside, and she was singing, I thought I was hearing a CD player, I was amazed to know that she was the one singing, and she was a Christian, at least she believed in Jesus and goes to church.

We became friends, we were so close, she was the only one we there for each other, until sexual pressures started creeping in, one day my dad came visiting and said "son, it is important that a young minister like you should get married so you do not fall into sexual temptations" I felt that word came right on time. I told Jenny, "Jenny I am not a kid, what I need is not a boyfriend girlfriend relationship, what I need at this stage of my life is marriage" though jenny obviously loved me, and I loved her, but she said she won't be ready until the next eight years, wow!

Right there I knew, we had to be real with each other and move on. Remember Jenny was the one that helped me when my dad passed on to glory. She was my confidant, but I knew if I should wait in that relationship we would be committing sin against God and our bodies; I Knew the devil will use it to destroy my future. I went into sincere prayers, cried out to God and said to God, if you do not want all the great visions you showed me to sink, please intervene quickly and connect me with the woman you have prepared for my destiny. The lesson here is never to allow sentiment and emotions make you comprise your destiny.

HOW I MET MY WIFE

After many prayers and consecration, the Lord started to work His work. My friend Ruth (not her real name) who was about getting married called me all from the blues, expressing urgency in her voice. It was the night of her engagement party, and the following day was the wedding. When she called, I was first reluctant to answer the call, but then the Holy Spirit prompted me to pick it up. The reason for not wanting to pick up the call is because I did not know why she would call me. Amid my struggles to connect with the right life and destiny partner, I was once in a relationship with her. I loved her and she loved me but the only mistake I made was, I never sought God's face as to if she was the one God had in mind for me. I must clearly state that there was no soul tie in terms of physical intimacy of any kind, just simply desiring to get married later in life until a faithful night, I and Ruth were coming from one of my ministrations and I heard the Lord say "she is not your wife" I froze when I heard this. This period was when I just returned from Abuja to Ilorin in 2003/2004.

However, I persisted with the relationship, but the same thing kept happening each time we were coming back together from any of my ministrations. I was heartbroken and she was too, because I had to let her know. We stayed as friends but not close enough to be intimate. So in 2006 November/December Ruth called me and asked me to please come and see her, it did not make sense to me but the Holy Spirit said go and see her so I obeyed. Not knowing what she would say, I saw that there were many people in their house, it was a wedding eve. So, she said she wished it was us but still the Lord asked her to tell me about someone who is a niece to her husband. At first it still did not make sense to me, I laughed about the idea, but she was serious about it and asked me to pray about it. After that day she kept calling to ask if I prayed, so in order not to lie, I prayed about it, shockingly one day the lord showed me in an open vison the niece of her husband that I have never seen before physically and her mom welcoming me to their house. It was a yes from God, so I told her that received a confirmation. My wife was studying in the US, so one a faithful day the uncle called me and introduced us and from the day I heard my wife's voice on the phone we never could stop talking. It was a divine connection from day 1. We got married in December 2017 to the glory of the Lord and it has been a glorious destiny ride ever since. This is our fifteenth year of marriage and blessed with three lovely children. God is good.

I WAS DENIED VISA

After the wedding day, which was a glorious day God proved himself and glorified himself to the point that people were praying to God that their wedding day should be that glorious.

Immediately we started processing my visa to join my wife in the US. I was denied the visa for reasons beyond our understanding. I knew there will be a need for prayers, we encouraged each other put in for another visa application immediately and even though it was expensive, God helped us. The waiting thus began and it was long, almost a year plus and was not easy. People were wondering and asking questions and it was during this period the Lord said to me "I have finished the work on your visa but go into the studio and record me one or two songs before you leave".

Since then, I stopped just waiting and I got busy with purpose because ursuit of purpose is one of the ways to conquer boredom, depression and discouragement while waiting on the Lord for what He has promised. At once I got into the studio and started recording. My wife came to visit Nigeria and we shot some videos together. That was when I recorded "loruko Jesu Iyanu yio sele" (In Jesus name there shall be a miracle) It was my visa situation that inspired me to write the song.

The song today is a prayer anthem in Nigeria and around the world.

I WAS GRANTED US VISA GREENCARD

Time went by fast, and the Lord said to me again "leave Ilorin and go to Lagos or Ibadan, Nigeria somewhere away from Ilorin, till I finish my work in you". Immediately, I moved to Lagos, Nigeria. It was then that the visa process picked up with speed and I was granted an interview and this time was a success. I received the Visa. The night before my flight to the US, I heard the Lord clearly and audibly "New York".

I called my wife and I told her. The following morning, I boarded the plane and flew to the US. I arrived in Atlanta and connected to Chicago where my wife was based. This was in 2009 and we stayed in Chicago for less than a year.

THE MISSION TO USA

Moving to the United States for me was like starting from the beginning again in a new territory. Everything was different. My songs that I recorded in response to God's instruction back in Nigeria had already started opening people's heart to my ministry in Chicago. Invitations started pouring in. On the interim because I could not afford to be idle, we started a monthly worship, Teaching and impartation meeting called Heart Print ministries, it was registered and there was a great impact. In one of my ministrations, I met some couple of ministers that are Nigerian Americans. Some of them are my friends since then till today. Ministerial relationships were birthed. A senior pastor walked up to me and expressed his desire for me to join his church, immediately I let him know that I have my calling and we will be moving to

New York, but in the meantime, I do not mind joining.

2009 /2010 December, the Lord spoke to me at home before the cross over service that the time for my Apostolic ministry has begun, that I should begin forty days fasting and prayer. That same night as we got to the church service the pastor told me the same thing word for word "the time for your Apostolic ministry to begin is now" I knew it was a confirmation that it is time for the ministry we have been processed for, for years and that it was time to move to New York to start the work. Few weeks later, my pastor asked me to keep coming to his house to be mentored for my new assignment and I did. Later we were prayed for and sent forth.

THE MOVE OF FAITH

Moving from Chicago to New York was a move from the familiar to the unfamiliar. It was a move from the known to the unknown. We had already bought a house in Chicago, which means we will have to think of selling the house because moving property that far was also not cheap. It was just I and my wife. We drove from Chicago to New York Syracuse to feel the place and our conviction grew even stronger we were full of joy and excitement for the work. We drove about 13 hours full of energy, singing to a CD playing praise songs to God all through. We knew nobody except an acquaintance of my wife of many years ago and his wife. Finally, we moved, we got a moving company who moved our properties from Chicago to New York, Syracuse. While we were still thinking of how to pay the moving company (they had not collected their money yet). Suddenly we received a call from the company that we should not bother to pay. It sounded unbelievable; it was nothing short of a miracle. We moved into a house where which could afford as at that time. This was a place our neighbor was a smoker and the smoke flows through the basement to our house. It was a tough beginning. Our car was repossessed. We were taking buses from home to work, from home to church. Our members were a couple (A brother and his wife) and us.

One day I took a walk and was wondering how the vision God showed me would come to pass, the vision of going to the nations of the earth to preach the gospel. I was wondering how people will know me in Syracuse talk less of the nations of the earth. A month after we moved God performed the miracle, my wife got pregnant after waiting for four years. We strongly believe that the miracle baby was as a result of our obedience to God's instruction to come to Syracuse New York.

LIBERTY CHRISTIAN WORSHIP CENTER WAS BORN

The same day the Church Liberty Christian Worship Center was inaugurated was the day we did the baby dedication of our first born. He is qualified to be called Liberty Baby to the Glory of God. Today through Liberty Global mission, the Liberty Vision has touched about 16 Nations and more across the Globe, from North to South America, West and East and South Africa, Asia, United Arabia Emirate, Europe and Antarctica. Liberty missions is legally registered and planted in four Nations of the earth (Nigeria, Ghana, South Africa and North America and Hopefully soon in the Philippines). Liberty Global mission operates a ministerial and leadership academy called Liberty Global Academy. Liberty operates a media outfit called Lib T.V and a bookstore called scepter bookstore.